ONLY ONE YEAR

Andrea Cheng

ONLY ONE YEAR

ILLUSTRATIONS BY Nicole Wong

LEE & LOW BOOKS INC.
New York

To Janis, with love —A.C.
In memory of Nana —N.W.

LEE & LOW BOOKS Inc., 95 Madison Avenue, New York, NY 10016
leeandlow.com
Manufactured in the United States of America by Worzalla Publishers, January 2010
Book design by Christy Hale
Book production by The Kids at Our House
The text is set in Aldine 410
The illustrations are rendered in ink, plus watercolor for the jacket
10 9   8   7   6   5   4   3   2   1
First Edition
Library of Congress Cataloging-in-Publication Data
Cheng, Andrea.
Only one year / Andrea Cheng ; illustrations by Nicole Wong. — 1st ed.
p. cm.
Summary: Nine-year-old Sharon has conflicted feelings towards her copycat little sister
and rambunctious toddler brother, who is sent to China for a year to live with relatives.
ISBN 978-1-60060-252-8 (hardcover : alk. paper)
[1. Brothers and sisters—Fiction. 2. Separation (Psychology)—Fiction. 3. Chinese
Americans—Fiction.] I. Wong, Nicole (Nicole E.), ill. II. Title.
PZ7.C41943On 2010   [Fic]—dc22   2009022786

CONTENTS

ONLY ONE YEAR

Not So Long

My little brother, Di Di, is sitting on the kitchen floor, emptying a cabinet. He takes all the plastic containers out and throws them on the floor. Then he starts on the pots and pans.

Mama is slicing zucchini for dinner. "Sharon, please take Di Di out of the kitchen," she says.

I'm busy making a card for my new friend Isabelle's birthday. She just moved in down the street. She's about to turn nine, and she's going into fourth grade, just like me. I draw a flag with

fireworks around it because Isabelle's birthday is on the Fourth of July.

"Mary, get Di Di," I tell my sister.

"You get him," she says.

"It's your turn," I say.

"Girls," Mama says. "Stop . . ."

Suddenly Di Di starts screaming. He's closed the cabinet door on his finger. Mama puts down her knife and picks up Di Di. She runs his finger under cold water.

"Shhh, Xiao Di Di," she tells him. "Shhh, Little Di Di. It's okay. Your finger is all better now."

"Better," Di Di says, rubbing his eyes. Mama puts him back on the floor and shuts the cabinet tight. Then she tells us that in two weeks she is taking Di Di to China to stay with Nai Nai, our grandma, for a year.

"A whole year?" I say. I can hardly believe it.

Mama begins frying the zucchini. "China is

better for little children," she explains. "In China Di Di will have Nai Nai and Auntie Jing and Uncle Tao and so many cousins to watch him."

"But here he has us," I say.

"You and Mary will be in school. Ba Ba stays late at work. I am starting my new job in the junior high school office. Who can take care of Di Di?"

"A day care place . . . or a babysitter," I say. "Amy across the street babysits."

Di Di is busy with the cabinet again. "Open," he says, tugging at a door.

"I have to work until four thirty every day," Mama says. She puts the fried zucchini into a bowl. "Di Di is only two. We cannot leave him with a stranger." She swallows hard. "A babysitter is not like Nai Nai. For a babysitter, Di Di is a job. But for Nai Nai, he is a grandson."

Mary starts crying. She doesn't want our brother to leave.

Mama holds her close. "Only one year. It's not so long."

Di Di carries two pot lids into the living room and starts banging them like cymbals.

"I still don't want Di Di to go," Mary says.

"I know, but sometimes it is the best thing," Mama says. "In the mornings, Nai Nai will take him to the market. Then after lunch your grandpa, Ye Ye, will take him to the playground on the corner. Di Di will learn to speak Chinese, just like you girls did when you went to China. Remember?"

I close my eyes. All I can remember about China are the photos in the album.

"A year will go by very fast," Mama says. "Then Di Di will come home to us again when he is old enough to go to preschool."

"A year is all of fourth grade," I say.

"And all of first grade," Mary says.

"Nai Nai will send pictures every week." Mama looks out the window. "We have to work, go to school. We cannot pay so much attention to our little boy." Her voice cracks. "We have to do what is best for Di Di," she whispers, "not what is best for us."

Leaving

For the next two weeks Mary tries to carry Di Di everywhere.

"He can walk by himself," I finally tell her.

"I know. But I want to carry him. He's leaving the day after tomorrow."

"You're spoiling him," I say.

Mary sits Di Di on her bed, and he reaches for her music box. He opens it, listens to the tune, and smiles. A ballerina is doing a dance in the box.

"Doll," he says, and tries to take the ballerina off its stand.

"Be gentle," I say.

He pulls harder.

"No," I say.

Di Di pushes the music box to the edge of the bed. It falls on the floor.

"You shouldn't let him break your stuff," I tell Mary.

She picks up the music box and opens the lid. It still plays music, and the ballerina turns. "It's not broken," she says. "And I can spoil him if I want to."

Di Di wears a blue sailor suit with a white hat. Mama has on a blue suit too, a jacket with a skirt to match. At the airport I'm afraid to say anything because of the lump in my throat. Mary clutches our dad's hand.

"Mama will be back next week," Ba Ba says, giving Mary's hand a squeeze.

Di Di stands at the window. His eyes dart all around. "A pa," he says, pointing to an airplane.

"*Fei ji*," Mama says, giving him the Chinese word.

Ba Ba buys each of us a soft pretzel. "Do they have pretzels like this in China?" Mary asks.

"They have other snacks," Mama says.

"Like what?"

"Plum candy. It's very good."

Mary scrunches up her nose. "I like pretzels better."

"How do you know?" I ask. "You've never tasted plum candy."

"Girls, stop bickering," Mama says.

Di Di has no idea what's going on. He's running back and forth in front of the window with his pretzel. When it's time to board, Mama picks him up.

"Say bye-bye to your sisters. Say bye-bye to Ba Ba."

Di Di moves his pudgy fingers to wave and drops his pretzel. "Bye-bye," he says, waving with both hands.

Ba Ba snaps a picture. I pick up the pretzel and put it in a trash can. Di Di doesn't know it will be a whole year before he sees us again.

PHOTOS

When Mama comes home from China, she brings us kitten slippers and a photo album for the pictures Nai Nai will send. Ba Ba puts the picture of Di Di waving at the airport on the first page.

"He's so cute," I say, pulling the album toward me to get a closer look. "I wish Nai Nai and Ye Ye had a computer. Then they could send us pictures right away."

"I offered to buy them a computer, and a digital

camera," Mama says. "But they said they like doing things the way they always have."

"Di Di didn't know he was going to stay in China," Mary says.

"What happened when you left?" I ask Mama.

"Ye Ye took Di Di to the park."

"So he didn't know you were leaving," I say.

"I told him." Mama looks down. "But he's too little to understand."

Di Di on a rocking horse. Di Di with Uncle Tao at the zoo. Di Di holding chopsticks. Every week Mary and I put the photos in the album. Then we sit on the edge of my bed and look through the pages.

"I like this one," Mary says one night, pointing to a picture of Di Di on a merry-go-round.

"His hair is getting thicker," I say.

Mary nods. "And he's taller."

I go check the calendar hanging in the kitchen.

"Thirty-nine more weeks until Di Di comes home," I report.

"Plus two days," Mary adds, closing the album.

SCHOOL SHOES

Mama takes us shopping for new school shoes. I pick out a pair of tan slip-ons.

"Those are not good for your feet," Mama says. "Shoes that tie are better." She picks out a clunky black-and-white pair.

"Nobody wears shoes like that," I say.

"If nobody wore shoes like this, they wouldn't have them in the store," Mama says. "Why don't you try them on?"

I put my feet into the shoes and stare at the mirror. My legs look even skinnier than usual. "I don't like them," I say.

"Me neither," says Mary.

Mama brings over four other styles for us to try, but all of them are big and ugly. "Girls in fourth grade don't wear shoes like that," I say.

"First graders don't either," Mary says.

Finally Mama lets me try the slip-ons. "They'll come off your feet when you run," she warns. "You'll trip and fall."

"Isabelle has shoes like this," I say, "and she can run."

"Look at these," Mary says. She is holding up a pair of small-sized sneakers with trucks on them. "These would be perfect for Di Di."

"Or these," I say, holding up tiny boots. "Aren't they cute?"

"Can we get him a pair?" Mary asks.

"We don't know his size," Mama says. "They might not fit."

Seeing all those little shoes makes my eyes tear up. Suddenly I want to leave the shoe store as fast as we can. But now Mama is looking at sneakers. "How about these?" she asks, holding up a blue-and-white pair.

I shove my feet into them. "They're fine," I say without even looking in the mirror.

Mary picks out sneakers that are just like mine, only they're pink and white. Mama pays for both pairs and we head back to the car.

We're quiet on the way home. Finally Mary asks, "Who will take care of us after school when you start your new job?"

"Mrs. Anderson will look in when you get home, and I'll be back a little after four thirty.

You girls are big now. You can be by yourselves for a short while after school."

"We'll be fine," I say, putting my head back against the seat.

GETTING READY

Mary says she's scared of first grade.

"You'll be the best in the class," I tell her. "You can already read better than most first graders."

"I'm not scared of reading."

"What are you scared of?"

"I don't know."

"I'll be in the same building," I say. "And your friends from kindergarten will be in your class."

"But I don't know where our rooms are," Mary says.

We sit on the floor, and I draw Mary a map of our school. I show her where the first-grade rooms are and how she can walk down the hall and up the stairs to get to the fourth-grade rooms.

"You'll be in room 102," I tell her. "I'll be in 202, right above your room."

Mama calls us to dinner. Mary folds the map and puts it in her pocket.

After dinner we set out our clothes for the first day of school. I decide on a blue skirt with a white top that has blue around the neck and sleeves. Mary wants to wear a pink skirt and a pink blouse.

"That's too much pink," I say.

"It's my favorite color."

"It's still too much," I say. "No one else in first grade will be wearing all pink."

Mary puts the pink top back in her drawer and takes out a white blouse with small yellow flowers.

"That's better," I say.

"Girls," Mama calls. "Get ready for bed. You don't want to be tired on the first day of school."

Mary crawls into bed with Bubby, her stuffed bunny, and falls asleep right away like she always does. I'm not tired. I look across the hall to Di Di's empty room. I wonder what he's doing right now. It's early morning in China. Maybe he's having noodle soup with Ye Ye. Or maybe he and Nai Nai are already at the market.

I close my eyes and try to sleep, but the room feels stuffy. With the blanket on I'm too hot, but without it I'm too cold. Even with my eyes closed I can still see colors: pink and blue and yellow. Maybe Di Di likes yellow best. When he comes home, I'll ask him.

First Day

Mama insists on walking us to school.

"We can go by ourselves," I tell her. "Or we can walk with Isabelle."

"I'll go with you on your first day," Mama says.

When we get to school, the yard is already full of kids. We go to where Isabelle and her mother are standing.

Mama starts talking to Isabelle's mom, and Mary is looking around. "Where do I go?" she asks me.

"See the numbers on the ground? Just find your room number, 102," I tell her.

"I don't see it."

"Over there." I point to the other side of the school yard.

"Where?"

Isabelle and I lead Mary over to the first-grade area, and Mary stands right on the number.

"Not *on* the number," I say, pulling her off. "You're supposed to stand next to it so other kids can see it."

Mary stands as stiff as a board. Mama comes over to us and looks at her watch. "I'd better go," she says. She kneels and puts her arms around Mary. "You're a brave girl," Mama tells her. "Try to remember everything you do so you can tell me when I get home."

Isabelle grabs my hand. "Come on," she says. "Let's find 202."

Near the fourth-grade area we see a girl saying good-bye to her little sister. "You have a little brother, don't you?" Isabelle asks me.

"Yup."

"Where is he?"

"At home," I say quickly. "With my dad."

My stomach flips. Why did I say Di Di was at home when he is halfway around the world? The words just came out of my mouth.

The bell rings, and we get in line behind our teacher.

Playing School

It turns out Mary likes first grade better than I like fourth grade. She chatters on and on about Ms. Martin and all the fun projects they're doing and how their first unit is on Native Americans. At the end of the unit they're going to invite all their families to a Native American celebration.

Every day after school I have lots of homework to do, but Mary doesn't.

"I wish Mom was here," Mary says one day. "Or

Di Di. Then I'd have someone to play with."

"There's not much you could play with a two-year-old."

Mary gets the photo album. "Want to look at the pictures with me?"

I shake my head no. I don't want to look at pictures of Di Di at the zoo and at the park and laughing in Ye Ye's lap. So Mary looks at them by herself.

Mrs. Anderson rings the bell a little while later. "How are you girls doing?" she asks when I open the door.

"Fine," I say.

"Let me know if you need anything," Mrs. Anderson says. "Your mother said she may have to work late today, but your father should be home in less than an hour."

"Thank you," I say. Then I take out my math book to start my long division problems.

Mary is watching. "What're you doing?"

"What's it look like? Stop talking or I'll never finish my homework." I write my name and the date at the top of my paper.

"You never want to play with me," Mary says. Her voice sounds hoarse, as if she might cry.

I take a deep breath. "We can play school," I say. "I'll give you some math problems."

"Okay," Mary says. "Addition. With two digits."

"And subtraction, with borrowing. Remember what I taught you last summer?"

Mary nods.

I write the problems on a piece of notebook paper. Mary does her work and I do mine.

"Time for gym class," I say when I'm done.

"I'm not finished yet," Mary says.

"Next time work faster." I take her paper. "First we have to warm up."

We do twenty jumping jacks. Then I show

Mary how to do a headstand against the wall.

"Good, but straighten your legs."

She does.

"Okay. Now come down and do it again."

We don't even notice when Ba Ba opens the door.

"Hi, girls," he says. "Nice headstand."

We start playing school every afternoon when I finish my homework. Some days Mary's bunny, Bubby, joins our class. He doesn't follow directions very well, so he has to sit in the corner a lot.

"What did he do wrong?" Mary always asks.

"He forgot to raise his hand," I explain.

"Ms. Martin doesn't care if we forget to raise our hands."

"I'm not Ms. Martin," I say.

The letter carrier brings the mail, but we are too busy to see if there is an envelope from Nai Nai.

MINIATURE HOUSE

The mornings are getting colder, so we wear our jackets to school. On the way home one day, Mary starts filling her jacket pockets with acorns.

"What are you going to do with them?" I ask.

"I don't know."

I pick up a tiny one. It looks just like a miniature spinning top. "Hey, I know," I say.

"What?"

"We can make a miniature house."

"Out of acorns?"

"You'll see."

Mary and I set up our house on the bottom bookshelf in the living room. We use matchboxes for tiny beds and make a desk out of toothpicks. "What about the acorns?" Mary asks.

"They're miniature toys."

Mary puts a few acorns by a couple of the beds so the kids can play with them when they wake up in the morning. We look in Mama's fabric box and find blue and pink velvet that's good for bedspreads. Mary cuts small rectangles. I place them carefully over the beds.

We add tables and chairs made out of cardboard and toothpicks, and lamps with acorn cap shades. Mary makes rugs out of yarn to put by each bed. I sew tiny pillows.

Ba Ba brings home more cardboard from his office that is perfect for walls and doors and a fireplace. He helps us cut the pieces straight with a utility knife so that everything fits together just right. Then Ba Ba puts in a tiny lightbulb that turns on and off with a switch.

Isabelle says it's the best playhouse ever.

"Our dad's an architect," I tell her. "He designs buildings and makes models like this all the time."

"Cool," Isabelle says, bending a piece of wire to make a chandelier. I make a sofa with stuffed cushions and a big chair to put in front of the fireplace. Every day we add more to the house.

Mama takes over the photo album. Each week she adds the pictures that Nai Nai sends.

"Come look at the new photos of Di Di," she says on a Sunday afternoon. But we are busy making a small bookcase with tiny books.

When the weather turns cold, we make snow from soap flakes and spread it all around the miniature house. Mama shows us how to make dough out of flour and salt and water. We roll the dough into balls and make a snow family for the front yard.

I use markers to draw the faces, and we glue on acorn hats. Mary gathers tiny twigs for the arms. Isabelle makes a snow dog and two puppies.

"I love the yard," Mama says. "The snow people and animals are very cute."

All through the winter we add more rooms. "Your house is becoming a mansion," Ba Ba says.

"The family has lots of children," Mary says.

"Yup. Like maybe sixteen," I say.

Ba Ba laughs. "That *is* a big family."

"I wish we had more kids," Isabelle says. "But my mom says one is enough." She looks at Mary and me. "You're lucky. You each have a sister."

Mary's eyes meet mine. We don't remind her about Di Di.

In March we clean off the snow, and Mary makes tissue paper flowers to put in the front yard. I cut out a cardboard tree and stick on small green leaves. Ba Ba helps me make a tire swing out of wire and electrical tape. We hang it from the lowest tree branch.

SPRING

Finally in April it turns warm. Mary and Isabelle and I walk up the hill to the playground and sit on the swings.

"My parents changed their minds," Isabelle says.

"About what?" I ask.

"One kid." She starts pumping the swing. "My mom's going to have a baby in October. We've already started decorating the room. I hope it's a girl."

"We have a little brother," Mary says. Then she covers her mouth with her hand, but it's too late.

"I forgot about him," Isabelle says.

"We call him Di Di, but his real name is David," I say.

"Where is he?" Isabelle asks.

"In China with our grandma."

"I visit my grandma sometimes. In Indiana. When's he coming back?"

"July," I say, pumping my legs so my swing goes higher than Mary's and Isabelle's.

Isabelle lets her swing slow down. "That's three months from now," she says. "How long has he been at your grandma's?"

"Since before school started," Mary says.

Isabelle is quiet for a few moments. "That's weird," she says finally.

"No, it's not," I say. "Anyway, China is better for little kids."

Isabelle pulls her eyebrows together.

I let my swing slow down to match hers. "In China he's learning Chinese. And there are lots of people to take care of him."

"Like who?" Isabelle asks.

"Grandparents, aunts, uncles, cousins. Not just some babysitter or day care place. And it's only for one year. He'll be back in the summer."

Isabelle jumps off the swing. "Our baby is going to stay home with my mom and dad and me."

A New Bed

The weather turns hot, and at the beginning of June school gets out for the summer. Mama has the summer off too, from her job at the junior high school.

Ba Ba works in the basement at night, building a new bed for Di Di. "He has outgrown his crib," Ba Ba says.

"How do you know?" I ask.

"He is already three," Ba Ba says. "You slept in a regular bed when you were even younger than that." Ba Ba measures a board and marks it with a pencil line.

I hold the boards while Ba Ba saws. After he drills holes in the corners, we take turns putting in the long screws. When the bed frame is finished, Ba Ba gives Mary and me sanding blocks and shows us how to sand with the grain of the wood until the wood feels smooth. That way nobody will get a splinter.

The walls of Di Di's room are pale green. "How about painting the bed yellow," I suggest. "I think that's Di Di's favorite color."

Ba Ba nods. "We have some yellow paint in the storage room."

"And maybe we could paint something special on the headboard," I say, "Like an airplane."

While Ba Ba gets the paint, I sketch an airplane on a piece of notebook paper. I make the nose pointed and the wings wide. I remember Di Di

at the airport, pointing to the airplane and saying "A pa." But he is bigger now. I wonder if he even likes airplanes anymore.

Mama sits at her sewing machine making a new green plaid bedspread. Mary wants to make a pillow to go with it. "Is this too small?" she asks Mama, holding up a scrap of the fabric.

"Not for a small pillow," Mama says. She shows Mary how to fold the fabric in half, sew down the sides, put in the stuffing, and stitch the pillow closed at the top.

"Do you think Di Di still likes airplanes?" I ask.

"I would think so," Mama says.

Ba Ba and I put two coats of yellow paint on the bed. When the second coat is completely dry, I copy the airplane sketch onto the headboard. Using a small brush and blue paint, I outline the whole plane. Then I fill in the body with a lighter shade of blue and paint the wings silver.

"You should write his name somewhere," Mary says.

I write "Di Di" across the top of the headboard in pencil, right below the plane. Then I trace over the letters with red paint and stand back to see how it looks.

"Great," Mary says.

The second "i" is a little shorter than the first, so I add to the bottom. "There," I say, putting down the paintbrush.

Home Again

Di Di looks so big when Nai Nai carries him off the plane.

"Xiao Di Di," Mama says softly. "Little Di Di." She tries to take him, but he grips Nai Nai's sweater in his fists and won't let go. Mama closes her eyes and takes a deep breath.

I pat Di Di's head, but he turns his face away and buries it in Nai Nai's sweater.

Ba Ba opens the stroller. Nai Nai puts Di Di in, but he starts crying. "I'll carry him," Nai Nai says, picking him up again.

"He doesn't remember us," Mary complains.

"Give him time," Ba Ba says. "And remember, he's very tired after the long trip from China."

I push the empty stroller as we walk through the terminal and into the parking lot.

When Mama straps Di Di into his car seat, he arches his back and tries to get out. I have to hold his arms while Mama clicks the buckles. Then he really starts crying.

"Look out the window," I say, pointing. "See the airplane?"

He stops for a minute. The plane is loud as it lifts up into the sky.

"Airplane," I tell him.

Then Di Di starts crying again.

At home Ba Ba and I show Di Di his new bed.

"Di Di," I say. "See the airplane?"

He stares at me.

"I think he forgot the English word," Nai Nai explains. "Di Di, *fei ji*," she says, touching the painted headboard.

He looks but won't let go of Nai Nai's skirt.

I try to hold Di Di on my lap and read him a story, but he bats the book away. Mary tosses him a red rubber ball. He runs to Nai Nai, and the ball rolls under his bed.

"He doesn't like us anymore," I say.

"It's not that," Ba Ba says. "He just has to get used to us again."

I go into the kitchen. Mama is slicing apples and arranging the pieces in a circle on a plate.

"Di Di didn't have to go to China," I say. "He could have stayed here with us."

Mama doesn't say anything.

"Or he could have just stayed in China. I think he liked it better there anyway." Then I'm sobbing.

Mama puts her arm around my shoulders, and I lean my head against her. "See the apple slices on this plate?" she says. "This is America, over here." Then she moves one of the pieces out a little bit. "And this is China, over on the other side. They are far apart, but they are all in one circle, like our family."

Mama hands me a kitchen towel to wipe my face. "We have to give him time, Sharon," she whispers. "He's been away for a year."

Nai Nai walks into the kitchen and sits at the table with Di Di.

"Apple," I say to Di Di. "Have some apple."

He looks at me from Nai Nai's lap.

"*Ping guo*," Nai Nai says. "Apple." She takes a slice and bites it. "The apple is very sweet."

I hand Di Di a piece. He stares at me for a few moments, then crams the whole apple slice into his mouth.

Looking for Nai Nai

Nai Nai can only stay for two weeks.

"I wish you could stay for a whole month," I say.

Nai Nai holds my hands in her wrinkled ones. "Ye Ye is in Shanghai, and uncles and aunties and cousins."

"But we are here," I say.

"I'll be back again," she says. "In the winter."

I look out the window. The trees are full of green leaves. "Winter's a long time from now," I say.

"Not so long," Nai Nai says. "You'll see. Time goes fast."

The first night after Nai Nai leaves, Di Di looks for her everywhere.

He opens the closet doors. "Nai Nai?"

He looks in the bed where she slept. "Nai Nai?"

"Nai Nai went bye-bye," I tell him. "We took her to the airport, remember? She went on the airplane."

Di Di doesn't understand, so I tell him the same thing in Chinese, but he still doesn't get it. He pushes a chair over to a window and climbs up.

"Nai Nai?" he says, looking out.

Mama holds Di Di so he won't fall. "It's okay," she says softly. She touches his cheek. "Nai Nai went to her home. This is your home. Here you have two big sisters and Mama and Ba Ba."

Ba Ba gets some paper and crayons and draws a

picture of an elephant to distract Di Di.

"*Zai hua yi ge,*" Di Di says, pointing to the picture.

"Another one?" Ba Ba asks.

Di Di watches while Ba Ba draws a whole line of elephants. Then Di Di starts to whimper, so Mama takes him outside. He gets quiet, staring at the streetlights. But later when Mama tries to put him to bed, Di Di cries and cries.

I close our bedroom door and stuff a rolled-up towel along the bottom, but Di Di's crying is as loud as ever.

Mary sits up in bed. "I'll give him Bubby," she says, holding him up by his ear.

"You better not," I tell her. "You can't sleep without Bubby."

"I can't sleep with Di Di screaming," she says.

I follow Mary into Di Di's room. Mama is in a chair, rocking Di Di.

Mary jiggles Bubby in front of Di Di's face. "Look, Di Di," she says. "Look. Bubby can dance."

Di Di stops crying. He reaches for Bubby.

THE PLAYGROUND

In the morning Di Di and Bubby follow Mary everywhere. She pretends she is the teacher and Di Di and Bubby are in preschool. First she gives him a crayon, and he scribbles a picture.

"Nice job," she says, and puts his drawing on the refrigerator. "Now it's time for gym." Mary does a somersault. Di Di tries to copy her, but he rolls sideways.

"Like this," Mary says, showing him how to tuck his head.

He tries again.

"Very good." Mary claps and Di Di claps too.

I pick up Di Di and sit him on my lap.

"Mary," he says, reaching for my sister.

I hold him tight.

"Nai Nai," he calls, starting to cry.

"You got him started again," Mary says. "Let me hold him."

"No," I say. I don't want to let my brother go. "Why are you playing school anyway? Didn't you ever hear of summer vacation?"

"I'll take him," Mama says.

I open the back door.

"Where are you going?" Mary asks.

I walk outside and let the door slam. I hear Mary running after me, but I don't wait. I wish I didn't have a little sister who follows me everywhere and a little brother who screams half the night. I wish I had a peaceful family like Isabelle's.

When I get to the playground, I hurry over to the swings. I kick off my sneakers and use my toes to climb up the pole. Mary does the same thing on the other side of the swing set.

"Stop copying me," I say when we get to the top.

We perch on the top pole, staring at each other.

"Di Di cries too much," I say after a while. "I wish he'd stayed in China."

Mary covers her mouth with her hand. She can't believe I said that. "He's our brother," she says.

I look down. The mud is dry and cracked around the puddles. "You think I don't know that?"

"He's just little," Mary says.

"You think you know everything about little kids?" My voice is loud. "Miss Know-It-All."

Mary slides down the pole and takes a drink from the fountain. Water squirts all over her shirt.

"You're making a mess," I shout.

"It's only water," she says, taking another mouthful.

"Don't put your mouth on the fountain," I warn. "You'll catch all the germs."

Mary looks up. "Stop telling me what to do."

Mary goes over to the edge of the baseball field and kneels down. She takes small bits of mud and rolls them around in her hands. Mama will not be happy when Mary comes home covered with mud.

I slide down the pole. "Let's go," I say.

Mary doesn't look up.

"Come on," I say.

She acts as if she doesn't even hear me. I head down the hill toward our house.

House Repairs

I open the screen door and listen for Di Di's crying, but it's quiet. Nobody's in the kitchen. I go into the living room.

Ba Ba is on his knees in front of our miniature house. The furniture is scattered all over. The staircase is broken. The tissue paper flowers are in little bits. An earthquake has hit our house.

"What happened?" I ask.

"Di Di," Ba Ba whispers. "He was looking for

you and Mary, and when he couldn't find you, he had a tantrum."

"Where is he?"

Ba Ba points to his and Mama's bedroom. I tiptoe to the doorway. Di Di is napping on the bed with Mama, his head resting on her stomach. They are both asleep.

Ba Ba has been trying to puts things back together, but he doesn't know that the pink bedspread goes in the blue room, not the pink one. He doesn't know that the bookcase is supposed to be in the living room. He doesn't know how to make tissue paper flowers.

Tears come to my eyes. "Di Di is a bad boy," I say.

"Shhh," Ba Ba says. "He doesn't know any better."

"You and Mama said China was better for little kids. But Di Di didn't learn not to break things."

"No matter where they live, most kids have tantrums once in a while. You had a few tantrums when you were a little girl," Ba Ba says, trying to reassemble the chandelier. "I think for now we should fix your house. And then we need to move it to a higher shelf."

I kneel down next to Ba Ba and hand him the tiny legs of a bed. He glues the pieces together carefully. We start on the stairs.

"But Di Di cries so much," I say.

"He's not crying now." Ba Ba takes a tiny piece of cardboard from my fingers.

Soon the miniature house takes shape again. The only thing left to do is make new flowers. Ba Ba and I try to make them out of tissue paper, but his look like lollipops and mine look like snowballs. Mary is better at making flowers than we are, but she still isn't home.

I go back up the hill, and Mary is standing in the middle of the baseball field.

"Mary," I shout.

She turns toward me. Her face is streaked with mud and tears.

"Come here."

"I can't," she says, pointing at a flock of birds pecking at the grass. "I'm scared."

"Of birds?" I can hardly believe it. "Just run."

But Mary is frozen. So I run out to the field flapping my arms and shouting, "Shoo! Go away. Shoo!"

The birds rise all at once and settle in the tops of the trees.

I walk over to where Mary is standing. She swallows hard. "There were so many of them."

"They're only birds," I say, taking her hand and leading her to the drinking fountain. I hold the foot pedal while Mary washes her hands and face and gets a drink. Then she holds the pedal for me. I dry my face with my shirt.

"Come on," I say. "We need your help. Di Di messed up our house."

"He did?

"Yup. He pretty much tore apart the whole thing. Ba Ba said he got upset when he couldn't find us, so he had a tantrum and threw everything all over the place. Ba Ba and I fixed the furniture and stairs and chandelier. But our flowers don't look right."

"You have to pull the petals apart," Mary says as we turn into our driveway. "I'll show you."

DUCKS

I peek into the bedroom. Di Di is just waking up. He whimpers for a minute. I hand him Bubby.

"Bubby," he says, sliding off the edge of the bed and following me into the living room.

Mary is inspecting the miniature house. "It looks pretty good," she says, moving the table over so it is centered underneath the chandelier. "Except for the flowers." She sits on the floor and cuts a strip of tissue paper, rolls it up, and pinches the bottom. Then she cuts small slits and pulls the petals apart.

Di Di is watching Mary. "*Hua*," I say, holding up the flower. "Flower."

"Flower," he repeats.

"What do you think we should make for summer?" Mary asks.

"I don't know. . . . Maybe a pond. With ducks." I go into the kitchen and get flour, salt, and water to make the dough. Di Di looks on as I mix the ingredients. I add a little more flour so the dough won't be sticky. Then I give Di Di a piece to play with. He squeezes it in his fingers.

I make five ducks from the soft dough: a father, a mother, and three ducklings. Mary cuts the pond out of blue paper and puts it in the front yard of the house.

"Ducks," I say. "These are ducks, Di Di."

"Ducks," Di Di repeats.

"A whole family of ducks," I tell him. "Ba Ba, Mama, Sharon, Mary, Di Di."

Di Di points to the ducks one by one, saying each name. Then he looks up at me. "Nai Nai," he says.

I pinch off another piece of dough and form a duck. "There's Nai Nai," I say.

"Ye Ye," Di Di says.

I make one more duck. Then we paint them yellow, with small black eyes and orange bills.

When the paint is dry, we put all seven ducks in the pond.

"Who is this?" I ask Di Di, holding up the littlest duck.

"Di Di," he says, pointing to himself.

THE ZOO

"Could we take Di Di to the zoo one day?" I ask Mama. "He liked the zoo in China, didn't he?"

Mama nods. "How about if we go tomorrow?"

I find Di Di playing in the living room. "Di Di, do you want to go see animals?" I ask.

He doesn't understand.

"Want to see the elephants?"

"Elephants," Di Di says, and runs to his room to get his sandals.

"Tomorrow," I tell him. "We'll see the elephants tomorrow."

The next morning we put a picnic lunch, a jug of lemonade, and Di Di's stroller into the car and set off.

Di Di likes the elephants even though he's scared when they lift their trunks. He likes the giraffes too, with their really long necks. Mary likes the hippopotamuses.

My favorite animals are the chimpanzees. We watch a mother chimp carrying her baby. "They're just like people," I say as she sets down the baby and starts grooming it with her fingers.

Di Di is getting impatient. He holds up his arms for Mama to pick him up.

"You can ride in the stroller. We brought it just for you," Mama says.

Di Di shakes his head no. He wants somebody to carry him. He starts stamping his feet. "Up," he says.

"I think in China there were so many people around all the time that somebody always carried him," I say.

Di Di goes to Mary. "Up," he repeats.

Mary picks him up, but after a few yards he gets too heavy and she puts him down.

"Up," he says. He looks like he's about to cry.

"You're getting too big to carry," Mama says. "You can walk like a big boy or you can sit in the stroller."

Di Di sits down on the path and refuses to move.

"He'll change his mind in a few minutes," Mama says. "Just ignore him for now."

"Look," I say, pointing at the chimpanzees. Two little ones are fighting over a banana. Finally the mother comes over and takes it away from them.

One sulks with its back to us, and the other one starts jumping around and screeching.

Mama laughs. "Good thing we don't have that baby chimp in our family," she says.

Di Di looks at Mama. He wants to know why she's laughing. He gets up and stands next to us.

"Banana," Di Di says, pointing to the mother chimp, who has moved to higher ground to enjoy her snack in peace.

We sit at a picnic table and eat our sandwiches.

"Ba Ba told me I used to have tantrums," I say.

"Most little kids do, but they outgrow it," Mama says.

"How old was I when I stopped?"

Mama tries to remember. "I'm not sure. Maybe somewhere around four."

"Di Di's getting better already. He didn't cry today," I say.

"Banana," Di Di interrupts. He is pointing to the area where the chimps are. "See banana."

I take his hand. "You want to go see the chimps again?"

"See the chimps," he says, pulling me along.

Book Bags

We all need new book bags for school. I pick out a big one since I will be in fifth grade. Mary takes a smaller pink one. Di Di wants the one with an airplane on it.

"That one is too big," Mama says. "Look, this red one is better."

"No," Di Di says, batting it away and grabbing the airplane one.

"You won't be able to carry this bag," Mama explains. "It's much too big for you." She takes the airplane book bag gently out of Di Di's hands and puts it back on the shelf.

"See," I say. "The red one has a smiley face."

"No," Di Di says, starting to cry.

"I'll take him outside," I say, grabbing Di Di under his arms to pick him up.

"Look at the concrete mixer," I say, setting him down once we are in the parking lot.

Di Di stares at the big yellow and red cylinder turning around and around on the back of the concrete mixer truck.

"Round and round," I say, moving my arm in a circle.

"Round and round," Di Di repeats, waving his arms around.

"The concrete mixer goes round and round," I tell him.

"Concrete mixer," Di Di says, but it sounds like "ke-ke misser."

We watch concrete spill to the ground for a new sidewalk. Men in big boots are smoothing it out flat. Di Di goes closer to watch.

"Ke-ke misser," he says.

One of the men looks up. "Concrete mixer? You're right, little guy," he says. "That big truck has a concrete mixer."

Di Di smiles.

When Mama and Mary come out of the store, we're still watching. "Ke-ke misser," Di Di explains to them. "Round and round."

OFF TO SCHOOL

On the first day of school I wake up before anyone and put on my new jeans, a striped T-shirt, and striped socks to match. I stand in front of the mirror. Is this the way a fifth grader is supposed to look?

I eat my cereal as fast as I can.

"Slow down," Mama says. "You have plenty of time."

"I want to get there early." I turn to Mary. "Hurry up."

"I'm hurrying," she says, gulping her milk.

"When do you go back to work?" I ask Mama.

"On Wednesday. The day after tomorrow," she says.

"Are you going to come with us on the first day, like you did last year?" Mary asks.

"I think you're both old enough to go alone today," Mama says.

Di Di is still in his pajamas, eating breakfast. When he sees me head for the coat closet, he climbs down from his chair.

"Me too," Di Di says, dragging his red book bag from the closet.

"You don't go to school today," I say. "Preschool starts tomorrow."

"Go to school," Di Di says.

Isabelle is at the door.

"Bye-bye," we say, waving to Di Di.

Big tears roll down his cheeks, but he doesn't make any noise.

When we get to the end of the driveway, I turn back. Mama and Di Di are at the door, waving.

"Your little brother is so cute," Isabelle says. "I can't wait until my mom has our baby."

"Just get ready. Little kids cry a lot," I say, taking Mary's hand as we cross the street.

As soon as Di Di sees Mary and me after school, he starts jumping up and down and shaking Bubby by the ear.

"Di Di's been asking for you all day," Mama says. "Each picture he drew was either for Sharon or Mary." She smiles. "None of the pictures were for Ba Ba or Mama."

Mama has made our favorite bean paste buns for a snack. Di Di stuffs one into his mouth, and red bean paste drips onto his shirt.

"You're making a mess," Mary scolds him.

"He can't help it," I say, getting a damp towel and rubbing out the stain.

"School," Di Di says when we're finished eating. He gets his red book bag and sits on the floor.

"Okay. Let's play school," I say. I give Di Di some paper and crayons. "You can draw whatever you want."

Di Di scribbles furiously on his paper. He pushes so hard that he breaks the red crayon.

"What are you drawing?" I ask.

"Concrete mixer," he says, and the words almost sound like "concrete mixer." Di Di holds the picture out to me. "Round and round."

"Good job," I say, and tape his picture to the refrigerator.

After we draw for a while, Di Di starts to rub his eyes with his fists.

"It's time for his nap," Mama says. "I tried to get him to sleep while you were gone, but he wouldn't even lie down."

"No nap," Di Di says.

"Everybody takes a nap at school," I tell him. I hold Di Di's hand and lead him into his bedroom. "Pick out a book for me to read to you."

He hands me a library book about trucks. "See the pickup truck?" I ask him.

He points to the picture. "Concrete mixer," he says.

"That's a pickup truck." I turn to the next page. "Here's a big concrete mixer truck," I say. But Di Di is already asleep.

Di Di's Book

Mary is waiting for me in the living room. "What do you want to do now?" she asks.

We should really do our homework, but I have an idea. We could make something for Di Di's first day of school. I try to remember preschool. There was a boy who was much bigger than me, and a jungle gym that was too high. But I loved story time.

"I know," I say. "We can make Di Di a book to take to school tomorrow."

We get more paper and some markers. Mary can

draw people better than I can, so she makes the cover with Di Di's face on it. I draw a yellow and red concrete mixer. Mary makes a duck family in a blue pond. I fold a paper airplane and tape it onto a piece of paper. Then I ask Mama if we can use some of the photos from Di Di's album. She says it's okay as long as we don't cut them up.

I look at Di Di on the first page of the album, waving to us from Mama's arms at the airport. "He looks so different now," I say, turning the page.

We choose a picture of Di Di with Ye Ye at the park, one of Nai Nai on the balcony of the apartment, and one of Di Di surrounded by some of our cousins. We tape the photos to the pages of our book and write the names underneath.

For the last page Mary draws Bubby with his floppy ears. We paste the cover picture onto a piece of cardboard, punch holes along one side, and sew all the pages together with yarn.

Dɪ Dɪ's Book, I write on the front, under the picture of Di Di's face. Then I put the book on the kitchen table and we start our homework.

About an hour later we hear Di Di making noise. I open the door to his room and see him sitting up, playing with a toy truck. His hair is every which way, and his cheeks are all pink from sleep.

"Di Di," I say, holding up the book. "We made you a present."

He sees the cover, smiles, and reaches for the book. I hold him on my lap, and Mary sits next to me. I open the book to the first page.

"Concrete mixer. Round and round," Di Di says. He turns the page. "Ducks," he says, pointing, and then names them all.

When we get to the photos, Di Di holds the book closer to his face. "Ye Ye," he says. "Nai Nai. Nai Nai went bye-bye."

"Yes, Nai Nai went bye-bye," I say.

Di Di suddenly looks sad.

"Nai Nai will come again," I say. "When it gets cold outside."

"Okay," Di Di says, and turns to the next page.

Di Di wants to read his book over and over. He shows it to Mama and Ba Ba. He reads it to Bubby. When it's time to go to sleep, he puts the book right by his bed.

"Tomorrow you'll go to school too," I tell him. "And you can take your book."

First Day for Di Di

"You are the slowest person I have ever seen," I tell Mary the next morning. "I mean, how long does it take to eat a bowl of cereal?"

Mama looks at the clock. "You still have time, Sharon," she says. "Go wake up Di Di, please."

I go into Di Di's room. He is lying on his side with his arm around Bubby. "Time to wake up," I say.

Di Di sits up, blinks his eyes a few times, and

then slides off the mattress. "Go to school," he says. He grabs his book and runs into the kitchen.

Mary is finished with her cereal. She is putting on her shoes about as slowly as possible.

Di Di gets his own shoes from his room and puts the left one on the right foot.

"The other foot," I tell him.

"By myself," he says, putting the right one on his left foot. He pulls the Velcro straps across. Then he stands and claps his hands. "Good job," he says, congratulating himself. He runs to get his red book bag, puts his Di Di book inside, and zips the bag shut.

Isabelle is at the door. "I came a little early so I could see Di Di," she says. "Hi, Di Di."

"Go to school," he says.

"He starts preschool today," I explain.

Mary is finally ready.

"Bye, Di Di." I say. "Have fun at school."

Di Di looks confused. "Go to school," he says, holding on to my leg. "Go to school."

"Mama will take you to your school," I tell him, but he won't let go. "You can't go to school with us. You're going to preschool." I unzip his book bag. "See. You can take your book," I tell him.

"Di Di's book," he says.

"Yes. You can show everybody the concrete mixer and the ducks."

Mama picks him up. "You girls better go," she says.

"Bye, Di Di," Mary says.

"Bye-bye," Isabelle says.

Di Di is trying not to cry. I hold his hand for a few moments. "Draw a picture for me at school," I tell him.

When we get home, I unlock the door with my key. Mama has left us a plate of cookies on the kitchen table. I take off the plastic wrap while Mary gets two cups and pours milk into each one.

Mrs. Anderson rings the bell. I open the door, and she pokes her head in. "How are you girls doing?" she asks.

"Fine," I say.

"Your mom should be home shortly," Mrs. Anderson says. "She went to pick up your brother." She smiles, waves, and then pulls the door shut.

Mary dips her cookie into the milk.

Suddenly the front door opens. There is Di Di, his book bag on his back and his Di Di book in his arms.

"Hi," I say. "How was school?"

Di Di puts his book on the table, climbs onto a chair, and sits down. "Cookie please," he says.

I give Di Di a cookie, and Mary pours him a cup of milk. She spills a drop and it lands on the table. Di Di puts his finger in the spilled milk and starts moving it around. "Concrete mixer," he says. "Round and round and round."

Mama comes into the kitchen with her camera. She snaps a picture of us to send to Nai Nai and Ye Ye.

"How did he do at school?" I ask Mama.

"When I went to pick him up, he was sitting on the floor with two other boys, looking at the book you made him. The teacher said he was fine all day, except he didn't want to take a nap."

"No nap," Di Di says. He dips his cookie into the milk just like we do and takes a big bite.

Swings

After we've finished our homework, I call Isabelle and ask her to come over.

"Do you want to go up to the playground?" Isabelle asks when she arrives.

"Sure," I say. "Can we take Di Di?" I ask Mama. Mama considers.

"Please," Mary says. "We'll be really careful."

"Okay," Mama finally agrees. "Put him in the stroller. And don't stay too long."

On the way up the hill, Di Di tells us about everything he sees. "Kitty," he says, pointing to Mrs. Anderson's big gray cat.

"Cat," I say. "His name is Storm."

"Storm," Di Di repeats, but it sounds more like "Torm."

"Sssss-torm," I say.

Di Di tries again. "Sssss-torm."

"Good job," I tell him.

"Birds," Di Di says, seeing the baseball field covered with birds. I remember how scared Mary was of the birds last year. But Di Di doesn't seem afraid at all.

We put Di Di in the little kids' swing and push him back and forth.

"*Geng gao*," he says, putting his head back.

"What did he say?" Isabelle asks.

"That means 'higher' in Chinese," I explain.

"Higher, Di Di," I say, giving him a harder push.

"Higher," Di Di says as he swings upward, his legs outstretched.

"He likes it," Isabelle says.

"He went to the playground a lot in China," Mary says. "With our grandpa."

"He's so cute," Isabelle says. "He makes me sort of wish my mom has a boy."

"A brother is fun, but I think a sister would be okay too," Mary says, getting onto one of the regular swings.

"I don't know about little sisters," I say, smiling.

Mary rolls her eyes.

Soon we are all swinging. Di Di is trying to pump with his legs like we do. I look out over the field. Down the hill is our house. If you turn left at the corner, the road leads to our school and Di Di's preschool, and to Mama's junior high and Ba Ba's office. Then, across the river, is the airport. And across the country and the ocean, far

away, is China. It's nighttime there. Nai Nai and Ye Ye are probably asleep.

"Higher!" Di Di calls.

I wait for my swing to slow down, then jump off. I grab the back of Di Di's swing and hold him over my head. "Ready?" I ask.

"Ready," he shouts.

"Are you sure?"

"Ready!" He kicks his feet and shrieks with joy.

I let go of the swing. Di Di's hair blows in the wind, and his laugh goes up to the treetops.

Author's Note

The idea behind this story may seem unusual, but it is not as uncommon as you may think. Some parents in the United States might find it hard to imagine being separated from their young children, but attitudes about raising children are sometimes quite different in other countries, especially in Asia and Africa.

Some immigrant parents who have young children in the United States send them back to their home countries for a year or two to stay with grandparents or other relatives. There are many reasons for making this difficult choice. Parents may find that they are unable to give their baby or very young child enough attention because they are busy trying to get started in a new country. They work, sometimes more than one job, and attend school, and try to save money both for their own futures and to support relatives back home. These parents feel it is better for a young child to be in a warm and loving environment with extended family members than in day care or with a babysitter. Day care and babysitters can also be expensive. Families are often unable to afford them and may not know about or be eligible for government services that might help them pay the costs.

Some families feel that little children are more restricted in the United States than in their home countries. They may come from villages where traditionally children are free to wander and the entire community looks out for all the youngsters. In addition, it is important to many parents that their children learn the language and culture of their home country and stay connected to their heritage. The parents hope that when their children are older, this knowledge will help them feel comfortable both in the United States and in their parents' native country.

The decision to send a baby or young child to live with relatives is never easy, and parents miss their children while they are away. However, these parents are making a decision that they feel is in the best long-term interests of their children. As they grow up, most children are grateful for these early experiences that allow them to understand two worlds.

Pronunciation Guide and Glossary

Ba Ba (bah bah): Dad

Di Di (dee dee): little brother

fei ji (fay gee): airplane

geng gao (gung gaow): higher

hua (hwa): flower

Jing (jing): person's name

Nai Nai (nie nie): Grandma

ping guo (ping gwo): apple

Tao (dao): person's name

xiao (sheow): little

Ye Ye (yeh yeh): Grandpa

Zai hua yi ge. (tsai hwa ee geh): Draw
one again. Another one.